The Quiet Evening

The Quiet Evening

BY THACHER HURD

Greenwillow Books, New York

Library of Congress Cataloging-in-Publication Data
Hurd, Thacher.
The quiet evening / by Thacher Hurd.   p.   cm.
Summary: As night falls, everyone and everything quiet down.
ISBN 0-688-10526-2.
[1. Night—Fiction.] I. Title. PZ7.H9562Qi 1992
[E]—dc20 90-24179 CIP AC

For Olivia

In our house,
Father and Mother
are sitting by the fire.

The sun has set,
and the faraway stars are shining
in the windows of our house.

Everyone is quiet.
Everyone is thinking quiet thoughts.

The clock is ticking softly—
ticktick   ticktick   ticktick.
The clock is talking to itself.

Far away, a river is running.
The river burbles and gurgles as it runs.
The river is whispering to its banks.

In our house, the fire has gone out
and no one puts any more wood on it.

Far away, the fish in the ocean
have all gone to sleep,
and a sea monster is resting
on the bottom.
The ocean has wrapped its arms
around all its fish
and sea monsters.

At home, our dog is asleep on the rug.
His paws twitch as he dreams
of running through fields
and sniffing under rocks.

Far away, someone has dropped
an anchor in the ocean,
and is fast asleep on a boat
that is gently rocking.
The waves slap the sides of the boat
as they pass by.

At home, Mother whispers,
"Good night, sleep tight."

Now everyone is quiet.

The clock is ticking,
the trees are rustling,
and the river is flowing.

The ocean is quiet,
the moon is shining,
and the earth is turning silently
in the starry night.

THACHER HURD wrote *The Quiet Evening* at the very beginning of his career as an author-illustrator of children's books. It was first published in 1978. Since then he has gone on to great success as the author-artist of such favorites as *Mama Don't Allow, The Pea Patch Jig,* and *Mystery on the Docks.* He and his wife Olivia founded The Peaceable Kingdom Press, which they own and run. They live in Berkeley, California, with their two sons.